CLAIMING ME

A DIAMOND IN THE ROUGH NOVELLA

REBEL HART

CHAPTER ONE

CLINTON

"Did'ja miss me?"

Rae hissed "Shit!"

I snickered as the librarian lifted her head. Rae's voice filled the space around us and she promptly slapped my chest. I grinned as I sat down next to her, my eyes darting between her and the books. It felt weird, not being with Roy during this free period. Usually, I sat with them on the porch of the cafeteria, despite our teachers' wishes. But today, after walking hand in hand into the school with Rae for the very first time, I sat with her in the library.

A place I'd never been my entire high school career.

Rae shook her head. "You're such an ass sometimes. You're going to get me in trouble with Mrs. Niche."

I blinked. "With who?"

"The librarian? The woman who's glaring at us right now?"

I grinned. "Didn't realize she had a name."

She paused. "Have you ever been in this library? Like, at all?"

"Do I look like the kind of person that's been in a library?"

"Are you ser—how are you passing your classes right now?"

"By the grace of Me."

She blinked. "You would attribute yourself to a god."

I grinned. "And you have no issues with that, do you?"

I reached over and tickled her, causing her to giggle. And before I knew it, a loud 'sh!' came from the front of the library. I looked over and saw Mrs. What's-Her-Face staring us down. With her finger to her lips and a frown on the edges of her face.

Rae pushed my hands away. "You're going to get me kicked out."

I shrugged. "That means we can go invade the stairwell."

She shot me a look. "I'm not going to that nasty place with you."

"We'd have privacy there if you did."

"There's no need for privacy at school."

"Does that mean we'll get some privacy after school?"

I grinned at her and she blushed. I loved it when she blushed. It tugged at a part of me before she stuck her nose back in those books. I sat there with my knee pressed against hers. I reached over and tucked a strand of hair behind her ear. She snickered and shook her head, gripping my hand as it slid down her face.

"Clint."

"Rae."

"I'm studying."

I grinned. "And you look very sexy doing it."

She rolled her eyes. "This part of the day isn't for you, dickweed."

"I love it when you talk dirty to me."

She scoffed, but a giggle still fell from her lips. The librarian shushed us again. I shot her a look. One that told her to shut the fuck up. Because if this was the only time I'd get with Rae today, I wanted to cherish it. I wanted to make it last. I wanted to create memories.

I wanted to do all of that with her.

"Come on. Let's get out of here, beautiful."

She sighed. "I have tests coming up. I have to study."

I tugged at her books. "You can study some other time."

She slapped her hand down onto them. "You need to study, too. We're in the same history class."

I paused. "There's a history test coming up?"

"You're kidding, right?"

And when I blinked, she sighed.

"Okay. You're studying with me."

"I'm what now?"

She giggled. "You're studying with me. Come on, Clint. Grades are important. And I'm sure yours are lacking."

The only important thing right now is you. "I'll study. Somehow, I always manage to scrape by on those things."

"And something tells me it's not because you know the material."

"Sh-sh-sh-sh-sh!"

I slowly panned my eyes over to the librarian whose name I didn't care to remember and glared at her. She glared right back, then put her finger to her lips and pointed to the door. And while I wasn't sure what the fuck she was trying to signal, Rae raised her hand. Waved at the woman. Like she understood, or some shit.

"What are you doing?"

Rae put her hand down. "If you don't shut up, we're out of here. And you're not going to be the reason I get kicked out of the library for the first time since being in this school."

I shrugged. "You're the reason I'm here for the first time. Why not repay the favor?"

She pushed me playfully and I smiled at her. A full-blown, cheesy-ass smile. This girl was growing in importance to me, and it kept taking me by surprise. I grabbed her hand and settled it against my knee. I scooted closer to her, peeking over her shoulder at her class notes. At the shit she had highlighted in her book. Rae, who had seen through all my bullshit and figured out who I really was, wanted to push me to start being better.

And I found I wanted to let her.

"Start reading here, then read right here in my notes."

I nodded. "Gotcha."

My eyes scanned the textbook, and already I wanted to fall asleep. I moved closer to Rae, my arm eventually slipping around her. If this was how I'd get closer to her, then so fucking be it. If I had to read some boring-ass shit about things that didn't have anything to do with me, I'd do it to be close to her. To feel her against me. To smell the scent of her conditioner and draw in her heat.

I sighed. "All right. Where in the notes?"

Rae pointed. "Right here."

"Uh, all those notes?"

"It's only half a page."

I sighed. "Fuck. Okay."

She giggled, then pressed a kiss to my cheek. And

every time I finished a portion of my reading, she kissed me. Again, and again. Pressing me on with rewards that made my stomach come to life. I grinned every time her lips touched my skin. At times, I turned my face and captured her lips with mine. A quick peck, nothing serious. But it was enough to make my cock throb against my jeans.

Rae giggled. "Focus, Clint."

I nuzzled my nose against hers. "I am, Rae."

"Aww, how cute."

"And they're studying together. So sweet."

"Was wondering where the fuck you got off to."

"Sh!"

Roy's and Marina's voices were punctuated by the librarian's. And as they came closer to us, I stiffened. I felt Rae press into me a bit, though she faced them head-on like the strong girl she was. I knew I'd made a mistake, not going to be with them outside. I knew I'd made a mistake in coming into this library instead of making my way for them. I mean, they were still technically my friends. And I'd technically bailed on them.

But I knew by the look on Roy's face this wouldn't be good.

"The hell are you two studying?"

Marina giggled. "Looks like something boring."

Rae sighed. "It's history, guys. We're studying for our history exam."

Roy quirked an eyebrow. "So this is where you

want to be? Studying some bullshit with some dumbass girl?"

I bristled. "You spend time with your dumbass girl all the time."

Marina grinned. "So she's your girl now."

Rae shook her head. "It's not like that. I'm just—"

I cut her off. "And if she is?"

Rae whipped her head around to look at me, and I saw the shock on her face. I mean, I got what she was trying to do. I knew what she was trying to do, actually. Write it off as some fucking tutoring session. But she didn't have to do that. We'd already walked into school hand in hand with each other. I'd already walked in with her and Michael and Allison.

No use in denying shit.

Roy sucked air through his teeth. "So this is how it's gonna be from now on?"

I sighed. "Do you need something? Or…?"

Marina scoffed. "I always told Roy you were an asshole that didn't give a shit about his friendship."

Rae paused. "What does Clint studying have to do with any sort of friendship? We have a test coming up."

Roy glared at her. "Looks like he's trying to shove his hand down your pants in the middle of the library."

Marina giggled. "Slut."

I rolled my eyes. "You're one to talk."

Roy bucked up. "What was that?"

I shot out of my chair. "Want me to say it a little louder?"

And as Rae stood up, sliding her hands up and down my arm, the four of us faced off in the library.

With the lazy-ass librarian shushing us from her fucking desk.

CHAPTER TWO

Roy grinned at me before he took Marina's hand. He tugged his girlfriend around us, and I watched them as they came around the table. They stood on the other side, behind the two empty chairs of the table. But they didn't sit down.

Rae sighed. "Get it over with so we can get back to studying."

Roy reached down toward the table. I saw him go for the book, but I reached out. I gripped his wrist before he could touch any of Rae's things. I eyed him hotly as he chuckled, ripping his hand away from mine. And like lightning, Marina moved for Rae's shit, flipping it off the table and onto the floor.

Roy smiled. "Good one, hot stuff."

Rae murmured, "Nice to know she's good at something other than sucking dick."

Marina whipped her head over. "What was that?"

I shrugged. "The truth."

Roy snarled. "You're walking on thin ice, dude."

I shrugged. "You've always been my thin ice."

He shook his head. "Where the fuck did your mojo go?"

Marina backed him up. "Yeah. What the hell happened to you?"

I quirked an eyebrow. "Are you about to throw a tantrum because I'm studying?"

Roy snickered. "You're doing more than that, and you know it. You think you can stand a chance at passing any classes with all the skipping you've already done this year? Talk about a fucking pipe dream."

Rae butted in. "His teachers will work with him. I'm sure of it."

Marina giggled. "Awww, how sweet. The little tramp standing up for her slice of meat."

Roy ran his eyes down me. "Not much of a slice of meat, if you ask me."

I grinned. "Says the boy who's self-conscious about his dick size."

Roy glowered. "What the fuck did you just say?"

Marina stepped forward. "I can vouch for the fact that—"

Rae held up her hand. "Ew. Please, don't."

Roy placed his hands on the table. "You're a snarky little shit, and that's all you'll ever be. No amount of studying with some chick you wanna screw's gonna get you past your senior year. Nothing. Might as well accept that and come back to where you belong. Because if you keep hanging around this freakshow? Your reputation is done around here."

Marina whined. "The girls miss you. Please, come with us."

I grinned. "That's cute, you begging. I see why Roy talks about it all the time."

Rae chimed in, "And outside of all this posturing, Clint has a perfectly reasonable chance of redeeming his grades."

Roy and Marina looked at one another, smiles crossing their faces. Then their laughter filled the space around us. Laughter so loud that other students started staring. Laughter so boisterous that the librarian actually got out of her chair. I peeked down at Rae and watched her blush. But, despite her embarrassment, she stood her ground.

Not once did she cave to them.

And I admired that about her.

The librarian cleared her throat. "If the four of you don't pipe down, you're banned from coming in here for the rest of the week."

Roy's laughter died down. "Promise?"

Marina smiled. "Good one, hot stuff."

Then Roy turned his attention to Rae.

"You leave him alone. It's not enough that you get to ride his cock like most girls in this school wanna do. You don't get to take my best friend away from me. You back the fuck off, got it, freakshow?"

Marina snickered. "Yeah. Go back to your own corner of the school. Clint'll call you when he needs his dick topped off."

I growled. "Fuck off, you two."

Roy smiled wildly. "Are you really gonna defend your fucking midnight booty call in the middle of the fucking library? The hell's happening to you?"

Marina shrugged. "She's probably got a tight one and he doesn't wanna lose it."

Roy turned his eyes to Rae. "Is it tight, sweetheart? Because I might wanna give that a try sometime."

Marina slapped his chest. "The hell are you talking about, asshole?"

Roy shrugged. "Hey. A man can play the field."

I rushed around the desk and grabbed Roy by his shirt.

"What the—?"

I snarled. "Let's get one thing straight, Roy. You're no man. You're a pathetic seventeen-year old boy who wants so badly to be cool. To be popular. To be part of the 'in' crowd. I'm not messing around when I said leave it alone. When I told you to leave her alone. Now, you can either do it, or you can suffer the wrath of what happens if you don't."

I released his shirt, shoving him so hard he stumbled back. Marina caught him, cooing softly in his ear like the momma's boy he really was. I looked at the librarian and saw her on the phone, murmuring to someone. Great. They'd ruined our fucking studying session. Rae and I would have to find somewhere else to go.

"Come on, hot stuff. Let's get out of here."

Roy pointed at me. "You're a fucking dead man. Got it?"

I stared them both down as they walked out of the library. Then I started packing up my things. I mean, I didn't have a lot of things to begin with. But the few things I had, I picked up. Rae hurried around me, stuffing her backpack full as the librarian sat down.

Because neither of us wanted to stick around for whoever she'd just called to intervene.

"Just ignore them, Clint."

I shrugged. "Sure."

She tossed her backpack over her shoulders. "They're nothing but insecure assholes who are afraid that you're going to leave them behind."

"Doesn't give them the right to talk to you like that."

"No, it doesn't. But I don't want them to get under your skin. Those aren't friends, Clint. And I hope you know that."

"Yeah, yeah. I know."

I made my way out of the library with Rae hot on my heels. I tried slowing my strides down since her legs weren't nearly as long as mine. But I needed to get this energy out of my system. I needed to jog around. Or take a nice, fast bike ride through the city. I needed to get my adrenaline pumping. I needed to get my body active.

I needed to burn off this fucking high I felt coursing through my veins.

"Clint, seriously. They're just threatened you're going to—"

I snickered. "Well, you're right. I am going to leave them behind."

She gripped my arm, stopping me in my tracks. "What?"

I sighed. "I am leaving them behind. I mean, at least I want to. I want to leave all this shit behind. Everything attached to this bullshit place. And I can't do that if I don't graduate."

Rae's face contorted. "Including me?"

The hurt that draped itself over her face made my stomach turn. I took her in my arms, holding her close as we stood in the middle of the hallway. I pulled her off to the side, into a little alcove that held a broken water fountain that hadn't been fixed in years. I leaned against the wall, feeling her sigh into my chest.

Then I pressed a kiss into the top of her head.

"You're the only thing making all this worth it, Rae. You should know that."

She nuzzled against me. "You just seemed so serious."

"Because I am. I want to get out of here. I want to get away from my father, and away from this school, and away from them."

She nodded. "But not me?"

I kissed her head again. "Never you, Rae."

And as if the world really, truly hated me, the bell for our last period sounded. Students flooded into the hallways as they scrambled for their last class of the day.

Rae pulled back. "I have to go."

"Come with me."

She paused. "What?"

I took her hands within mine. "Skip last period with me."

She furrowed her brow. "You want to graduate and get out of here, but then you want to skip class?"

"Just this once. After this, you have my word I won't skip."

She quirked an eyebrow. "Your word?"

I rolled my eyes. "All right, all right. You have my promise that I'll try my hardest not to skip."

"That sounds more like you."

I grinned. "So, are you in?"

She resisted. "I shouldn't."

"Even if it gets us some alone time?"

She paused. "Is your father not home?"

"Nah. Him and my stepmother are on yet another trip. Business or pleasure, I don't really know. The point is, they're not home. She's probably racking up some credit card on shoes and he's probably locked himself in a room making more money than he knows what to do with by bitching at people and scaring them into doing shit."

"What does your father actually do for a living?"

"I just told you."

She giggled. "You're crazy, you know that?"

I tugged on her hands. "So are you coming or not?"

And after a sheepish grin, she nodded.

"Lead the way, handsome."

CHAPTER THREE

W e burst through the front doors of my father's home, unable to keep our hands off one another. I kicked the door closed behind me, furiously grappling for more of Rae's kisses. Her lips felt like a thousand butterfly wings against my skin. Her tongue tasted of sunshine and the gum she'd been chewing on. I gripped her hips, pulling her closer to me. And as she slid my leather jacket off my shoulders, I took liberties that should've waited until my bedroom.

"Come here, gorgeous."

My growl made her groan, and it ignited some-thing inside me. I whipped her around, pinning her to the door as I stripped her down. Her naked body, free for me to take in. Her curves, free for my hands to roam. Her thighs heated. Her cheeks flushed. She gasped every time my lips touched her skin, causing my girth to leak for her. She tore my shirt over my head. I pulled my belt out of its loops. And once we were clad in nothing but skin, I gripped the backs of her thighs.

"Jump for me, beautiful."

She locked her legs around me and our mouths fell against one another again. My tongue fell to the back of her throat, teasing her and stroking her as I walked us up the steps. She shivered against me. Her puckered peaks pressed tightly against my muscles. Oh, how wonderful she felt. How warm and inviting her body became. My knees grew weak with every step up the stairs I took. Eager to get to my bedroom. Eager to get to my mattress.

Eager to have her underneath me.

"Clint. Oh."

We burst into my bedroom and fell to my mattress. She opened herself up for me, her legs parting to reveal to me those dew-dropped lips of hers. I kissed down her neck, raking my teeth against her pulse point. And as I fell to my knees, I tossed her legs over my shoulders.

"Hold on to whatever you want."

Her hands gripped my hair and I dove between her legs. Her taste overwhelmed me. Her smell intoxicated me. I lapped up her slit, gathering her essence on the tip of my tongue. And with every swallow, she marked me on the inside. She bucked against my lips. Rolled against my stubble. I growled as she groaned. I grunted while she moaned. I wrapped my arms around her toned thighs, pulling her closer. Needing my body coated in her as sunshine battered through my windows.

I wanted to drown myself in her.

"Oh, Clint. Shit. Don't stop. Right there. Right there. Left. Left. A little to the—yes!"

Her body pulled taut and she quaked against me. My mouth covered the entirety of her pussy, drawing from her every droplet of juice she had for me. I slid my hands up her thighs. Over her hips. All the way up to her tits, where I massaged them to painful peaks. My tongue worked her, throwing her over the edge yet again as she choked out my name.

"Oh—fu—Cli—nt."

I wanted to keep going. I wanted to keep tasting. I wanted to keep exploring. But she finally pushed me away. Her shaking body shook my mattress as I kissed the insides of her thighs. Nibbled on their dollops of excess playfully. My length ached for her. My body screamed to be inside her. But what I wanted was to cherish her. Spoil her.

Make her feel amazing.

I kissed both of her lower lips. I slowly kissed up her torso, playfully nibbling along my journey upward. She jumped and giggled, causing me to suck marks on the places where she was most sensitive. She darted beneath me. Told me 'no' and 'stop' while pulling me closer. I marked a trail with my lips. A trail that led straight to her mouth. A trail I'd memorize sooner rather than later.

A trail that showed me exactly how to please this incredible girl.

"Clint."

My name was nothing but a whisper. As she pulled me down to her lips, I felt myself become one with her. Her legs wrapped around me, trapping me between her thighs. I felt her rocking against me, coating me with her juicy heat. I felt the animal inside me rearing its head. Growling, ready to be let out of its cage.

And when her nails curled into my skin, the lock on the cage popped.

"You're mine."

I flipped her over and lifted her hips into the air, bringing her ass close to me as I slid deep against her walls. I gripped her hair, wrapping it around my knuckles and pushing her cheek into the mattress. My comforter muffled her wails as I thrust into her, feeling her walls tighten and expand to make room for my intrusion.

I snarled. "That's it. Just like that."

My thrusting became pounding. Her ass jiggled for my viewing pleasure. I held her up, keeping her face pinned to the mattress as her walls caved in around me. Her whimpers hit my ears. She pressed her hands into my bed. She bucked against me, begging for more friction like the good little girl she was. It robbed me of my breath. How tight she was for me. How warm and amazing her body had become to me. A heady sensation filled my body, making me feel as if I were flying.

I ascended to some sort of heavenly plain as her walls caved around me.

"I'm coming! I'm coming! I'm coming!"

I tugged on her hair, lifting her face out of the mattress. Those two words filled my room as she chanted them over and over again. I stuffed her body full of me. I felt every part of her dripping over my thighs. I pulled out and flipped her back over, spreading her legs as I hovered over her. The wolf in me reared its head. I felt my eyes widen as I gazed down upon my prey. With her voluptuous breasts bouncing against her chest and her legs spread wide for me, she looked like the perfect meal.

Rae.

My Rae.

Spread for me and ready for the taking.

I gripped myself and slid back inside her. I tossed her legs over my shoulders and folded her in half. Her eyes rolled back. Her hands wrapped around my wrists. And as she lay there, pinned underneath me, she quickly came again.

"Clint!"

And again.

"Fuck!"

And then, yet again.

"Shit, shit, shit, shit, shit."

Her voice grew hoarse as her legs slid from my shoulders. My balls hung low, aching for the release they'd been begging for. My face fell to the crook of

Rae's neck. I felt her sweating and trembling. The heat of her body pulled sweat to my brow as my hands found hers. I intertwined our fingers, resting my tuckered muscles against her body. I pinned her hands above her head, opening her up even further to my assault.

But instead, my hips moved slowly.

My body rocked gently.

And as we rolled in tandem, I couldn't take my eyes off hers.

"You're beautiful."

"Clint."

"The most beautiful thing I've ever seen."

"I can't—I'm so tired. Clint, I—"

I kissed her lips. "Just lay there and let me handle it."

I gazed into her brown pools of exhaustion and grinned. I grunted as her walls clamped around me, pulling me quickly to my own end. I kept my strokes soft, feeling her languidly wrap her legs around me. Her eyes fluttered closed and I nuzzled her, silently begging her to open them.

"Let me see you, Rae."

Her eyes fell back open and my heart skipped a beat. I knew I was getting myself in deep with this girl. I mean, I'd never felt this way. Sex had never felt this way before. And I didn't want to stop.

I wanted to keep going until she couldn't take it any longer.

Time blurred, our bodies entangled around each other. We rolled around with her legs straddling me before I flipped her back over. We drenched ourselves in sweat. The entire room smelled like us. And as I held her to my body with my back against the headboard, I thrust quickly against her.

"I'm close. Rae. I just—"

"Come with me. Please, Clint. Don't hold back."

My eyes rolled back and my legs locked. Her walls quivered around me, coaxing me to my high as my heart raced. Rae bit into my shoulder, muffling her cries of pleasure as we unraveled together. Clinging to one another, with her nails raking down my arms.

"Fuck, Rae."

She collapsed against me and the pumping of my cock finally stopped. I held her close to me, gasping for air as she shook and shivered. I stroked my hands up and down her back, kissing her shoulder as her lips fell against my pulse point. She kissed me, tiredly. Over and over again.

As my girth stayed sheathed within her body.

I could really get used to something like this.

And as those words fluttered across my hazy mind, I slid us down to the mattress, guiding her off to the side. I pulled her close to me, amazed that she let me manipulate her body.

Never had someone trusted me so much. Never had someone collapsed against me like that. Like a foundation they needed. Like the strength they required. Her lips fell against my ear as we wiggled underneath the covers, and the panting of her breath filled my body with electricity.

Oh, yeah. I could really get used to this.

Then Rae kissed the shell of my ear before she drew in a steady breath.

CHAPTER FOUR

"You don't need to keep throwing punches, you know."

Rae's voice wafted against my ear and I closed my eyes. Usually, something like this was nothing but a hookup. A way to pass the time when I didn't want to be in school. But as I held her close to my side, I stroked my fingertips up and down her back. I felt her leg sliding between mine. I felt her arm wrapping around my body, holding me close to her luscious curves.

It made me want to open up to her.

"I know. I know I don't. They just rile me up so bad."

Rae kissed my cheek. "I know they do. They rile everyone up. You used to pull that kind of shit, too. But you're not in this alone anymore. You've got me. You don't need to keep fighting your way through shit. Not if you don't want to."

I shrugged. "Fighting's all I know."

"It doesn't have to be, though. Clint, you're smart."

I snickered. "You're delusional."

She sat up. "No, really. You're smart. Deep down beneath all that insecurity and all that nonsense you hold up to the world, you're intelligent. Driven. Capable. Independent. You have all the tools necessary for someone to really make something of themselves. You just have to stop relying on your anger to take the steering wheel."

I grinned. "Are you trying to give me a pep talk?"

She shook her head, staying serious. "No. I'm not. I'm trying to get you to see your worth. Because something tells me you've never seen that before."

"Rae, you don't have to expend this kind of energy. Just come back here. Lay down with me."

"Not until you look me in my eyes and let me know you've really heard my words."

I rolled my eyes, but followed her command anyway. And the second our eyes connected, I felt paralyzed by fear. Her eyes were gorgeous. Filled with determination and care. I'd never had anyone in my life who gave enough of a shit to say these things to me. So, naturally, it scared the hell out of me. All sorts of things ran through my head. She slowly came back down to my body, pressing those glorious tits of hers against my chest. And as she smiled softly at me, I saw a horrifying image.

Rae continuously skipping classes with me. Finding her solace beneath my body as her grades continued to slip. I saw us riding my bike after I purchased her a leather jacket to keep her body safe. Riding away from school and off into the sunset. It was a picture that should have made me smile. A sentiment that should've made my heart skip a beat.

But I was paralyzed by an idea that rushed through my head. A voice, as stark as my father's, that chastised me for what I'd just made Rae do.

You'll drag her down with your endless bullshit.

I sighed. "I'm no good and you know it."

Rae kissed my lips. "Hush now. Hush that nonsense."

I shook my head. "I've always known this. It isn't anything new. My father's told me enough times—"

"Your father's a shithead whose word shouldn't be taken even with the grain of salt most people's word is."

"I don't deserve a girl like you."

"I don't give a damn what you deserve. This is about what I want as much as it is about what you want."

I felt myself shutting down. I pulled my eyes away from her and stared at the ceiling. I unraveled my arm from her and locked my hands together, then slid them underneath the back of my head. I wanted to sink into that mattress and drown myself in the covers. Anything to get her out of my bed and away from me. Holy fuck, I'd made her skip class. Rae. The girl who always studied. Who always aced her tests. The girl who could fucking nap through her classes and still pass them.

I'd made her skip class.

Because you're a piece of shit influence, Clint.

Rae lay down beside me. "I'm not going anywhere, Clinton."

I scooted away from her, but didn't say anything.

"No matter how much you pull away, I'm always going to be there."

She pressed herself against me again, but I moved. We continued that little dance until I was against the edge of my massive bed. And when she propped herself against me, she tucked her head underneath my chin. She pressed her ear against my heart. She wrapped herself around me, seducing me with her softness and her heat as I tried to steel myself against her.

Then she whispered, "This feels good, doesn't it? Right?"

I sighed. "Sure."

"So why would we want to give this up? Why would *you* want to give this up?"

Because I'm no good for you. "Because what's done is done."

"Not a cuddle-after-sex kinda guy?"

And when she giggled, my heart leapt with joy.

I'd never get used to that sound. I'd never get used to how nice it sounded. How easygoing it made me feel. I slowly unlocked my hands against my better judgment and let my arm drape around her. Softly. Tenderly. Foreignly. I'd never felt this way about a girl before. No one had ever been more than a hookup. More than someone to fuck and dump. But Rae was different. I mean, she'd always been different. But now? She was truly different.

A game-changer.

And one I found myself not taking lightly.

"Penny for your thoughts?"

Her voice pierced through my inner roll and I cleared my throat.

"Just thinking."

She kissed my chest. "About…?"

I shrugged. "Stuff."

"And things?"

"And other things."

She kissed my chest again. "Sexy things?"

I quirked an eyebrow. "Wait, are *you* thinking about sexy things?"

She grinned up and me and I wrapped my arms around her.

"Come here, you dirty little girl."

I pulled her up to me and pressed kisses all along her face. She laughed out loud, filling my room with the sweetest sound I'd ever heard as I rolled her over. I pinned her beneath me, her legs spreading as I kissed her up and down her neck. Her cheeks. Across her forehead as she tried shoving me away.

"Clint! That tickles! Cut it out!"

"But you taste so good, Rae."

"Clint! Mercy! Uncle! I give, I give, I give!"

My forehead fell against hers and she cupped my cheeks. I lay there, pressed against her curves that poured into the slats of my body. I breathed the air she afforded me. My eyes danced between hers. And as I sank deeper into her softness, I felt my heart stop in my chest. Butterflies took off in my stomach. I felt my iron-clad bones softening toward this girl. This awkward bookworm I'd teased and tortured all through high school.

How the fuck did I pull this off?

I dropped my lips to hers, kissing her softly. Things were moving fast—very, very fast between the two of us. But it didn't feel wrong. That was the kicker. It should've felt wrong. The girl I'd bullied suddenly wanting to straddle my body. The girl I'd tortured suddenly wanting to help me through school. The girl whose life I'd made a living nightmare suddenly wanting to be on the back of my bike. It should've been wrong. Everything pointed to it being wrong.

But, as she slowly rolled me over, only one word came to my mind.

Perfect.

I slid my tongue across the roof of her mouth. I slid my hands up and down her back, listening as the birds chirped outside. The afternoon sun streamed through the curtains of my room. And Rae? Well, she made the softest little sounds that made my cock come alive again. I parted my legs, feeling her slide between them. I sucked on her lower lip as her heart hammered against mine. Our lips fell away and her cheek pressed against my shoulder, her body seeking its home against mine.

Home.

Is this what home feels like?

"How much longer do we have?"

Rae's voice pierced my thoughts. Again.

"As long as you want."

She nodded. "Just making sure you didn't have anything going on."

I have nothing without you. "Nah, I'm good."

Then she nestled into me. Leaving her mark upon my thoughts—and my heart.

What the hell had this girl done to me?

CHAPTER FIVE

Two Weeks Later

I heard the loud sports car pull into the driveway and groaned. Dad and Cecilia were back from whatever trip they'd been on. I heard the front door slam open and I rolled my eyes. Even after two weeks of lounging around in the sun and working, Dad could find a way to come in and be an absolute sourpuss asshole.

But something inside me wanted to go downstairs.

Maybe it was Rae's positive influence. Or her insistence that this world gave a shit about me. Whatever the drive, I found myself standing in front of Dad while he slammed cabinets and murmured to himself about having no tea in the house.

When the fuck did any of us drink tea?

"How was your trip?"

He froze at the sound of my voice. "What?"

I cleared my throat. "How was your trip? Productive, I hope?"

He peered over his shoulder. "Sure."

"Where did you two go again?"

"There a reason I'm getting the third degree from you?"

I shrugged. "Just curious, I guess."

"Well, get less curious."

I paused. "So no to the talking about your trips?"

He slammed his mug onto the counter. "Clint, if there's something you need or want, spit it out. Because I've still got some important things to get done even though we're back."

And I'm not important. "Nah, I'm good. Just checking in on you."

He harrumphed. "Fine. Cecilia!"

She piped up behind me. "Yes, Howard?"

I whipped around, startled by her presence. Had she been standing behind me the entire time? Silent like that? Without saying a fucking word?

"You going out like that for our date night? Or are you changing?"

I paused. "Date night?"

Cecilia nodded. "I'm just changing really quickly. I figured I could shower at the suite after dinner."

Dad sighed. "I'd prefer if you showered here. Just make it quick."

"We'll miss our reservations if I do that."

"Which is why I said make it quick."

I murmured, "I'll leave you two to it."

"Oh, and Clint?"

Dad's voice gave me pause. "Yep?"

"Don't wreck the house while we're gone. We should be back tomorrow morning."

I nodded. "Got it."

An hour later, Dad was bitching up a storm as he and Cecilia left the house. They were back in his noisy-ass sports car, zooming off into the distance without having been home for more than a couple hours. And I had a craving to take my bike out for a spin. I needed to get out of this house anyway. It had been tainted by my father, and I needed to give the house time to breathe.

But the faster I rode, the more my thoughts spun.

Of course he wouldn't have time for me.

He's been gone practically four weeks! And I'm not important enough to talk to when he gets back?

You've never been important to him, Clint. Get over it.

I wish I was important to him…

I zoned out while driving my bike. And I didn't come to until I pulled into a parking lot. I stared at Grady's Groceries, watching through the window as I spotted Rae, standing at the cash register scanning groceries with the fakest smile on her face. I grinned at her presence. I pulled my bike into a parking space under the shade of a massive tree. One random tree in the middle of a small patch of Riverbend. My thoughts turned to her. How beautiful she was. How much I enjoyed being around her. She'd become my soft place to fall. Solace, in my time of need. Something I'd always needed, but never felt I deserved.

In some ways, I still didn't feel as if I deserved her.

I turned my bike off and slung my leg over. Putting down the kickstand, I leaned against it, my ass falling against the side of the leather seat. As I watched her through the windows of her work, the minutes ticked by. She had the closing shift today, and I knew how much she hated closing. Working those long hours after being at school all day. Still, she looked as if she were taking it like a champ.

Like the strong girl she had become.

I'm so fucking lucky.

Rae was special. The more time I spent around her, the more I was convinced of it. The more time I spent with her, the more I wanted to sequester more of her time. I wanted to own her. Have her as mine for as long as she'd let me. I mean, there were times where I could happily spend the rest of my days making Rae smile and taking care of her.

You got it bad, Clint.

And the thought made me smile.

Maybe one day she'd get on the back of my bike and ride off into the sunset with me. Not because she'd failed her classes and needed to get away. But because our future after school aligned that much. I loved it when she rode on the back of my bike. Her arms wrapped tightly around my waist. Her thighs squeezing me tightly as we accelerated down the open highway. The winding back roads of our hometown. Her laughter, making me all warm and fuzzy inside.

She's got you fucked up, dude.

I pushed away from my bike and started for the store. My hands fell away from my chest, swinging beside me as I walked through the automatic doors. A mindless greeting fell from her lips as she looked over toward me. But when her eyes connected with mine, a genuine smile crossed her face.

And all thoughts of my father faded into nothingness.

Finally, I'd found someone who felt like home. Someone who gave a shit about me. Someone to cherish me. Who enjoyed me. Who saw my worth, even when I didn't see it myself. I walked toward her as her smile grew bigger. I leaned against the end of her register, listening as the last of the customers walked out of the store.

Then, gazing into her eyes, I made myself a promise. The only promise I'd ever made myself outside of leaving my father's house the second I got out of high school.

I promise you, Rae, I'll do anything to keep you at my side. To keep you safe. To help you succeed in all the ways you want.

Because I just couldn't lose her.

It simply wasn't an option.

KEEP READING RAE AND CLINTON'S LOVE STORY:

Book 1: getbook.at/playwithme
Book 2: getbook.at/promiseme
Book 3: getbook.at/staywithme

RATE/RECOMMEND CLAIMING ME ON GOODREADS

ABOUT THE AUTHOR

Rebel Hart is an author of Dark and Contemporary Romance novels. Her debut novel, Play With Me, is the first book in a planned trilogy.

NEVER MISS A NEW RELEASE:
Follow Rebel on Amazon
Follow Rebel on Bookbub

Text REBEL to 77948 to don't miss any of her books (US only) or sign up at www.RebelHart.net to get an email alert when her next book is out.

autorrebelhart@gmail.com

CONNECT WITH REBEL HART:

ALSO BY REBEL HART

For a full list of my books go to:

www.RebelHart.net

www.ingramcontent.com/pod-product-compliance
Lightning Source LLC
Chambersburg PA
CBHW032045180726
48284CB00008B/2764